LAKE PRESS

Lake Press Pty Ltd
5 Burwood Road
Hawthorn VIC 3122 Australia
www.lakepress.com.au

First published 2017
Printed in China 5 4 3
LP19 376

NATIONAL
LIBRARY
OF AUSTRALIA
A catalogue record for this
book is available from the
National Library of Australia

Santa, I can Explain

Heath McKenzie

Santa, I can explain...

... I wasn't trying to find what my sister bought me for Christmas...

I was trying to find the best gift idea for her!

And I think I found it...
She'd love a new outfit!

And maybe a new phone too!

And I get the feeling Mum could do with a nice new vase...

... Although maybe this one did just need a wash!

As for my Dad... he's always so hard to shop for!

... But I'm beginning to think his beloved fish tank might be due for an upgrade!

Or maybe a new car might
be a good idea!
Can you fit a new car
on the sleigh?

Can I leave it up to you to think of the perfect gifts for the policeman (and his horse!)?

Not to mention
old Mrs Jensen,
Ralph the greengrocer...
and the local
children's choir?!

To be honest,
Dad's such a great guy —
he deserves a new fish tank
    AND a new car
    (if that's not too much trouble)!

But cancel the vase,
I'll think of something else for Mum!